KU-409-639

Sometimes

For Monika, and all those who feel with intensity! ~ S S

To everyone who has a rainbow in their heart,
knowing that a rainbow needs both rain and sun ~ E P

With special thanks to Dr Naira Wilson
for her help with this book.

LITTLE TIGER PRESS LTD,
an imprint of the Little Tiger Group ·
1 Coda Studios, 189 Munster Road, London SW6 6AW
www.littletiger.co.uk
First published in Great Britain 2021
Text by Stephanie Stansbie
Text copyright © Little Tiger Press 2021
Illustrations copyright © Elisa Paganelli 2021
Elisa Paganelli has asserted her right to be identified as the illustrator
of this work under the Copyright, Designs and Patents Act, 1988
A CIP catalogue record for this book is available from the British Library
All rights reserved · ISBN 978-1-78881-878-0
Printed in China · LT/1800/0098/1220
2 4 6 8 10 9 7 5 3 1

The Forest Stewardship Council® (FSC®) is an international,
non-governmental organisation dedicated to promoting responsible
management of the world's forests. FSC® operates a system of forest
certification and product labelling that allows consumers to identify
wood and wood-based products from well-managed forests and other sources.

For more information about the FSC®, please visit their website at www.fsc.org

Sometimes

STEPHANIE STANSBIE   ELISA PAGANELLI

LITTLE TIGER

LONDON

Your body's full of **feelings**:

like the tide, they ebb and flow.

Sometimes they lift you high

and sometimes they bring you low.

When cold, dark **fear** takes over,
it can swell up like a wave.
So pause and when you're ready . . .

take a leap, go on – be brave!

When your heart beats with
excitement,
and you don't want it to end . . .

a sudden **disappointment**

can be hard to patch and mend.

And when the day is gloomy
and you're **bored** and feeling glum . . .

just jump and dance, and soon you'll find
your **happiness** will come!

It's tough to be **embarrassed**,
cheeks burning hot and red,
with lots of awkward feelings
bouncing round inside your head.

Then **anger** overwhelms you,
bringing words you know are bad.

Or maybe you feel sorry
and your heart feels
small and **sad**.

And when you're feeling **lonely**
and lost and out of place . . .

a simple act of **kindness**

brings a smile to your face.

When you **forgive** another,

and you let bad feelings go . . .

then **peace** will fill your body
with a warm, contented glow.

So, hand-in-hand together,

you'll be feeling **safe** and strong.

Returning home to family,
the place where you **belong**.

Of all these many feelings
love is strongest through and through.
It swells up in my heart
when I cuddle close with you.

Sometimes we feel sad or scared or angry.

And that's fine! Everybody has these feelings.

Here are some ways to help you through these tricky times.

Anger

Anger is an energy and you need to let it out! Just try to make sure you do it in a way that won't hurt you or those around you. Use your words, ask for some space or go outside and run around!

Sadness

No one can be happy all of the time. So when you're sad, let yourself feel it for a while. And, once you're ready, soothe yourself! Play with your favourite toy or have a cuddle. Do the things that make you really happy.

Loneliness

You can feel lonely even when there are lots of people around. Ask someone if you can join in their game, or offer to share a toy. And remember, playing on your own can be really fun too.

Fear

Fear can stop you doing all sorts of things. But, if it won't hurt you, you should try and do it. Remember times you were afraid and faced your fear. Think about how you'll feel when you've done the scary thing – pretty amazing!

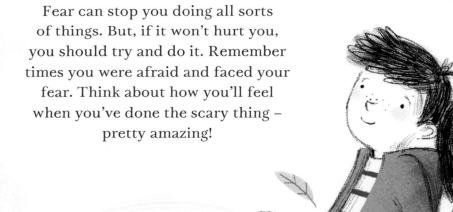

Disappointment

It can be so hard to get over a disappointment. When you're ready think about all the really good things you have, like your family, friends or a special toy. Imagine letting go of your disappointment as if it were a balloon. Then plan your next adventure!

If your child is struggling with an emotion, tell them you understand why they're feeling like they do – that you would feel that way too. Name the emotion and let them stay with it for a moment, before suggesting how they can deal with it when they feel ready.